Ten Creepy Monsters

ABRAMS BOOKS FOR YOUNG READERS
NEW YORK

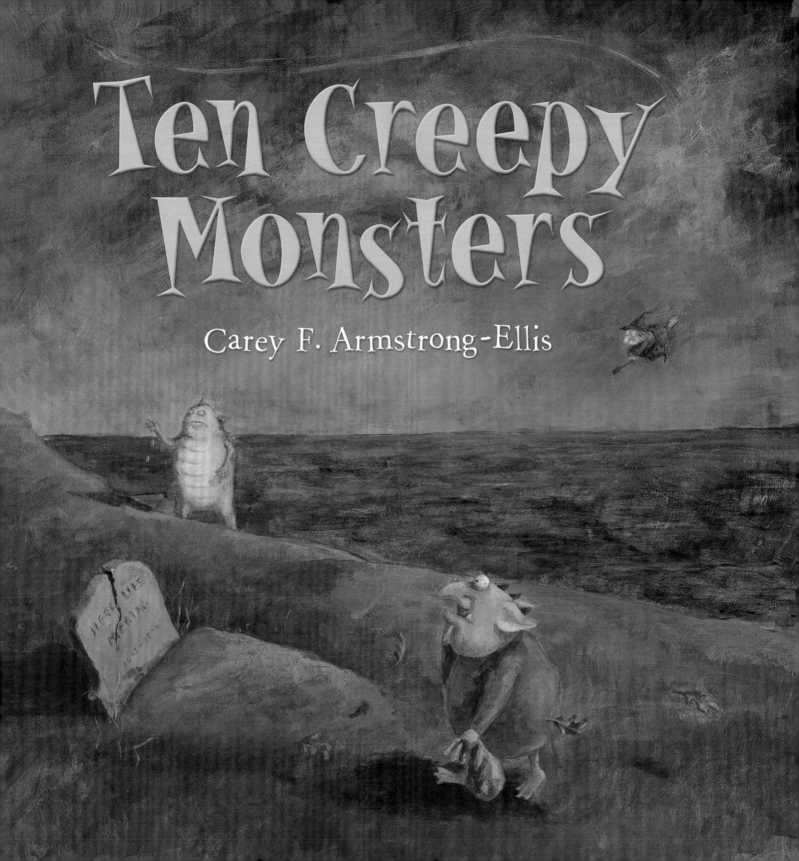

Ten creepy monsters met 'neath
a gnarled pine.

One blew away,
and then there were nine.

Nine creepy monsters trudged with lurching gait.

One lost his foot,
and then there were eight.

Eight creepy monsters gazed up at heaven,

One stopped to howl,
and then there were seven.

Seven creepy monsters
gathered up sticks.

One lit a match . . .

. . . and then there were six.

Six creepy monsters donned suits for a dive.

One found his love,
and then there were five.

Five creepy monsters crept through an old door.

One snagged his wrap,
and then there were four.

Four creepy monsters were dancing with glee.

One stomped too hard,
and then there were three.

Three creepy monsters stirred steaming swamp brew.
One spilled a bit . . .

. . . and then
there were two.

Two creepy monsters
were still having fun.

One saw the sunrise . . .

. . . and then there was one.

One creepy monster rushed home at a run.

He pulled up his blanket,
and then there were none.

To my groovy dad, who instilled in me a love
of B movies and cool monsters

THE ILLUSTRATIONS ARE ACRYLIC ON PAPER.

Cataloging-in-Publication Data has been applied for and may be obtained from the Library of Congress.
ISBN: 978-1-4197-0433-8
Text and illustrations copyright © 2012 Carey F. Armstrong-Ellis
Book design by Maria T. Middleton

Printed and bound in China
10 9 8 7 6 5 4 3

Abrams Books for Young Readers are available at special discounts when purchased in quantity for premiums and
promotions as well as fundraising or educational use. Special editions can also be created to specification. For details,
contact specialsales@abramsbooks.com or the address below.

ABRAMS
THE ART OF BOOKS SINCE 1949
115 West 18th Street
New York, NY 10011
www.abramsbooks.com